The My and the Whistling Teeth

Martin Waddell

Blackie

British Library Cataloguing in Publication Data
Waddell, Martin
The mystery squad and the whistling teeth.
I. Title
823′.914 [J]   PZ7

ISBN 0-216-91423-X
ISBN 0-216-91422-1 Pbk

The Blackie Publishing Group
Bishopbriggs, Glasgow G64 2NZ
Furnival House, 14/18 High Holborn
London WC1V 6BX

Printed in Great Britain by
Thomson Litho Ltd., East Kilbride, Scotland

Are You a Good Detective?

To solve this case you have to follow the trail wherever it leads you and spot the clues on the way. Some are in the story, some are in the pictures. If you crack the clues first time you get maximum points and end up with a Sherlock Holmes Detective Rating. If you don't, you may find further clues to help you but Beware of Custard Pies!

Add up your points as you go along and check your final score against the Detective Rating Chart on page 95. You'll find out how good you really are!

A book for Rebecca and Adam

The Mystery begins here . . .

1

'No detective work whatsoever. Understood?'

Casey's dad puffed his pipe at us, looking as if he might send the caravan up in flames any minute. He was dressed like a flower show in a summer shirt that Casey's Mad Grannie gave him. He had baggy shorts and red socks and rambling boots, though the only rambling he'd done in the week we'd been at Red Bay was down to the chip van to get our chips. We didn't mind him being bone idle, because it kept him out of

our hair. Now, quite unexpectedly, he had started playing the Anxious Dad.

'None of your Mystery Squadding!' he said, stealing a quick glance at the clock. 'Buzz off out of here and do the things normal kids do on holiday, without getting anybody arrested or finding treasure or kidnapped millionaires. I've had enough of life as a hard worked copper, thank you very much. I want some peace.'

'Yes, Dad,' said Casey.

Then Casey winked broadly at my brother James. Casey's dad had started talking about being a policeman again, which showed the way his mind was working. Detective-Inspector Peters was back on the job and we knew for sure that something was up!

'Scarper!' Casey's dad said, trying to make it sound casual, when all the time he was obviously itching to get us out of the way so that he could get on with whatever it was he wanted to get on with.

We knocked off down to the beach on our bikes with his '*See you at one-thirty sharp and NOT BEFORE THEN*' echoing after us.

'What's your dad spotted, Casey?' James asked.

'Something he doesn't want the Mystery Squad mixed up in,' said Casey. 'That's for sure!'

'When you think of all the mysteries we've solved for him . . .' Beans muttered bitterly.

We were all cheesed off, it wasn't just Beans. There are four of us in the Mystery Squad. Casey Peters is our Chief because he knows all about Solving Mysteries and my brother James Bacon is our Technical Expert. My name is Bodger Bacon and I am in charge of all Case Records and TSM (which means Top Secret Material) and the only totally useless member is my sister Beans, the one who looks like something a dinosaur sat on.

'Right!' I said. 'Mystery Squad Alert! Anybody spotted anything suspicious?'

'We're not supposed to be doing any detective work, remember?' said James. 'Casey gave his word, and his word goes for all of us.'

'This isn't detecting,' I said. 'Not *exactly*. Just thinking. We're not going to *do* anything.'

'Yet,' said Beans.

'At all!' said Casey, sharply.

'Any Special Observations?' I said, whipping my TSM notebook out of my saddlebag. A good detective should have a notebook handy at all times, because you never know when something will happen that ought to be noted down, and may later prove to be the Vital Clue in a big case. Sometimes I forget my book, but usually I don't. I opened it up.

PLACE:
Red Bay Camp Shop

OBSERVATION:
Possible Till Trick

SUBJECT:
Shop Man

OBSERVED BY:
Me

'The camp shop!' I said.

'What about the camp shop?'

'Bodge spends most of his time in there stuffing himself!' said Beans.

I could have told her I was keeping the shop man under surveillance, but I didn't. Instead I showed her my notebook.

'Big deal!' said Beans.

'What does it mean?' said Casey.

'It means the shop man keeps the front of his till covered with a notice about fishing boats, so that you can't see what he's ringing up,' I said. 'I think he rings up less money than he's putting in, and keeps the difference himself!'

'Good spotting, Bodge,' said James.

'I had to spend a lot of money buying things when I was doing it,' I said, hopefully. 'Sweets, and crisps and things . . .'

'And he wants a refund from Mystery Squad Funds!' said Beans.

'NO DICE!' said everyone, and Casey added: 'You ate 'em, you pay for 'em.'

'What have you lot spotted, then?' I said, indignantly.

'I spotted you stuffing yourself,' said Beans.

'Shut up!'

'I've noticed Dad talking to Mr Silver, the camp security man, once or twice,' said Casey.

'He was down looking at the Devil Divers' boat today,' said James. 'You know, the one those sub-aqua people use to take their diving gear out to Whistling Island.'

Nobody had anything important enough to go into my notebook.

'Right,' I said. 'Here is my deduction! The Devil Divers Club aren't real sub-aqua men at all but diamond smugglers and they are smuggling diamonds in their boat and Casey's dad and Mr Silver the security man are on to them and there is a big police swoop planned for this afternoon and there may be a real gangster gun battle on the beach and that is why your dad wants us out of the way.'

'Idiot,' said James.

'Go and jump in the sea, Bodge,' said Beans. 'Better still, we'll chuck you in.'

That was when I scarpered.

In the end we got on our bikes and went down to the Quarry Holes for a swim. We were still there at one-thirty!

'Your dad will go mad!' I told Casey, and we zoomed off across the sandhills which were great for rough riding and wheelies but not for getting straight back to the caravan.

Casey's dad didn't go mad.

He didn't go mad because he wasn't at the caravan when we got back.

'That's odd,' said Casey. 'You know the way Dad is about sticking to arrangements. . .'

'I don't like it,' said James. 'The place is too tidy.'

I knew what he meant. If our mum and dad had been able to get away from our chip shop and come with us instead of Casey's dad the caravan would have been cleaned up every day, but Casey's dad said he had enough to do tidying up all year after Casey, without doing it on holiday as well. Casey's mum is dead, so Casey and his dad have to look after themselves. Casey says his dad is very fussy at home but holidays are different.

1

'Maybe he wanted us out of the way so he could tidy up?' said Beans, but she didn't sound as if she believed it.

'He said we'd all tidy up, last day,' I reminded her.

'Nearly ten to two,' said James, checking his compass watch.

'Nobody tell Casey's dad we were late, and then he won't . . .' Beans's voice trailed away in mid-sentence. She was looking at Casey and James.

'Some sort of struggle?' said Casey. 'The clock gets broken. Somebody tries to clean up afterwards, trying to hide what's happened . . .'

'A broken clock can't prove all that, Casey,' James objected.

Then Casey pointed out the clue that had suggested a struggle to him in the first place.

Spotted the clue?

If you need help to find it turn to section **34**.
If you think you know the answer turn to section **47**.

2

'Please Mr Policeman, Casey's dad's late home and we want our lunch.'

No evidence to go to the police with, and Casey's dad was only half an hour or so late. He wouldn't be pleased if you made a fuss over nothing. Turn to **26** and consider the other options.

3

"Fifteen Men on a Deadman's Chest
Yo-Ho-Ho- and a bottle of rum!"

Turn to **15** and consider the options.

4

Right! You spotted it. Turn to **70**.

5

Wrong. Go to **58** and think again.

6

Bodger was right . . . but how did he know?
If you know the answer turn to **39**.
If you need help turn to **30**.

7

Wrong. Turn to **70** and try again.

8

You've fallen into your own elephant trap. Turn to **71**.

9

Wrong. Move to **21**.

10

You're guessing! Turn to **74** and try again.

11

Bodger's tip—re-read **1**. Got the answer? Turn to **14**. If you haven't, you may as well go there anyway.

12

Wrong. Go to **52** and have another try.

Detective Rating

4 points if you got here straight away!
Deduct 1 point for each wrong choice!

13

'The Secret of the Spanish Gold is that there isn't any!' said Casey.

'What?'

'You mean . . . you mean someone got here before us?' I said.

'No. There isn't any. There never was any Spanish Gold. It's a fairy story.'

'The Mystery Squad on Treasure Island!' groaned James. 'We've been set up.'

'Sent off like kids to hunt for treasure. Tricked by a *fake* map scratched on a rock . . .'

'Fake?' It was my map, I'd found it, and it didn't look fake to me.

'Not a very clever fake, either. In the bed of a stream . . . with small rocks tumbling over it all the time . . . scratching at it, wearing it away,' said James. 'The water alone would have worn the surface of the stone smooth.'

'That would take years,' I objected.

'It was supposed to have been there for years,' said Casey. 'The Big Foot should have given me the tip off, but I didn't think!'

'Big foot?' said Beans. 'What big foot?'

'The stream where Bodger found the stone map,' said Casey. 'There was a footprint—a large footprint. Much larger than Bodger's.'

'Porky?' said Beans.

'He planted a map for us to find, so we'd go running off up the Skull Rock . . . out of the way so the Divers could get on with whatever they're doing . . . while we were being treasure hunters, like kids in some silly story!'

'So Porky set us up,' said James.

'Or somebody else?' said Beans.

'Or Porky and somebody else?' I said.

Who dunnit?

Porky? Turn to **36**.

Somebody else? Turn to **41**.

Porky *and* somebody else? Turn to **82**.

Detective Rating

Score 3 points if you spotted the lie about Casey's mum.
2 points if you needed help.

14

Casey's mum is dead.

Which meant Porky was lying.

Which meant . . . ?

'He could be in their caravan!' I said.

'Or on their boat!' said Beans.

'Or on Whistling Island . . . or anywhere else, by now,' said Casey.

'What do we do?'

Usually Casey is the one who knows what to do, and we all waited for him to say something, but he didn't. He was looking really sick, which wasn't surprising. As he'd already said, it was his dad that was in trouble this time, not anyone else's.

James took over.

'One: we get help. That means we get on to Mr Silver, the camp security man, and ask him to get the police. Two: we put a watch on the Devil Divers' caravan . . .'

'He won't be there,' said Casey bitterly. 'They couldn't risk it.'

'They may have had to,' said James. 'All this happened in broad daylight, you know, and from the look of things your dad didn't give in without a struggle.'

'Moved in the car,' said Casey. 'Easy. All they had to do was get him in and drive off.'

'They didn't do that!' I said.

Who is right?

Casey thinks his dad was moved in the car. If you agree, turn to **81**.

Bodger says that isn't what happened. If you agree, turn to **6**.

Detective Rating

If you realised that there had to be two tall people in the party score 2 points. Deduct 1 point if you needed a clue and 1 point for each wrong choice.

15

'It won't work,' I said.

'Why not?' said Casey.

'The watcher will be expecting to see two *tall* people and one *small* person carrying the stretcher,' I said. 'If we come out with two *small* people and one tall one, he's likely to smell a rat.'

'He's right,' said James. 'For once.'

'What do you mean, for once?' I said, indignantly.

Casey didn't like it, but he had all three Bacons against him. Beans because she wanted to do the exciting bit herself, and James and I because we didn't want to give the game away.

We managed the stretcher easily enough, with James and I belting down to the camp talking loudly about Beans's terrible accident, and coming back with a tent and two tent poles, which were to be the stretcher, and the other equipment hidden inside. The dummy was easy . . . what wasn't easy was carrying it down the face of the Skull Rock!

If we'd dropped the dummy, we'd have given the whole game away.

We worked our way down to the original camp site, set up the other tent and carefully put the dummy Beans inside.

'I'm glad that's over!' I said.

'Let's hope Beans is on her way by now,' said James.

Casey didn't say anything.

He was turning over a piece of paper in his hands.

'What's that?' James asked.

'It's the code note that you and Beans left for us at the caravan,' said Casey, slowly.

'What are you looking so worried about then?'

'There's something written on the other side,' said Casey. 'Look.'

'So what?' I said, looking at it blankly.

'It's a page from your dad's notebook, isn't it?' said James, squinting at it. 'Beans must have found it lying round the caravan.'

'It's Dad's all right,' said Casey. 'That's what bothers me! We knew Dad was working on something, and this looks like a clue to what it was.'

'Doesn't look much like a clue to me!' I said.

'S.A. bullion job,' said James. 'South Africa . . . S.A?'

'Gold bullion,' said Casey. 'I think I remember Dad going on about it . . . but that's ages ago. Still, if it was the South African gold bullion job . . .'

'Spanish Gold!' I said.

'Nope, South African.'

'Gold, just the same,' I said.

'There's an exclamation mark, as if Dad was making some sort of joke, and then a question mark, as though he wanted to think about it.'

'What's L.J. then?' said James.

'And parrot?' said Beans.

'Parrot,' I said. 'How about Birdy?'

'Birdy?'

'That woman, Birdy Hamill. It could be a clue to her name.'

Casey suddenly went green! 'Oh no!' he said. 'I don't believe it. We've fallen for it, hook, line and . . .'

'Silver!' groaned James.

'I thought it was gold we were worried about,' I said.

'It has to be Silver!' snapped Casey. 'Don't you see? L.J.? Parrot? *Silver . . .*'

What's the connection?

The bullion job? Turn to **45**.
The Whistling Teeth? Turn to **57**.
Pirates? Turn to **61**.
Devil Divers? Turn to **77**.
Need a clue? Turn to **3**.

16

If the man on the stairs nabs you anything could happen . . . particularly if he's mixed up in the kidnapping. This time the sensible sounding thing isn't sensible, because the consequences if it goes wrong could be so serious. Turn to **59** and think again.

17

Dew you get this tip?
Turn to **52**.

18

Wrong! Turn to **82** and try again.

19

Right. But how do you know?
Bodger's tip: Look at the picture strip in **46**.
Got it? Turn to **72**.

20

Wrong! Go to **48** and think again.

21

You have been custard pied.
Go to **61** and try again.

22

Wrong. Go to **80**.

23

Right! But what *did* the message mean? Turn to **74**
when you've worked it out.

24

Wrong. Go to **52** and have another try.

25

Think again. Go to **60**.

Detective Rating

3 points if you spotted The Listener *by T.C. Assette straight away.*

2 points if you only succeeded in finding it with the aid of the clue.

Deduct 1 point for each wrong choice you made initially.

26

It was James's idea to conceal a tiny cassette recorder in the middle of a book. He'd got the idea from a book on smugglers in his crime library. I invented *The Listener* by T.C. Assette and Beans made the cover . . . it's really brilliant!

I switched to playback. We all listened.

Nothing.

Then:

'I'll thank you children not to play sneak tricks on me!' Casey's dad's voice came crisply over the tape, followed by a click.

'Serve you right, Bodge!' said Casey, with a grin.

'How was I to know he would spot it?'

'You shouldn't have done it at all, Bodge,' said James. 'Casey promised his dad we'd do no detecting . . . and the first thing you do is to switch on the cassette recorder and spy on *him*. I ought to thump you, Bodger.'

'What do we do now?' Beans asked.

'On the basis of the evidence so far,' said James, 'we . . .'

Well, what would you do?

You don't know what's happened to Casey's dad, but you strongly suspect that he had discovered something which called for further investigation.

Would you go straight away to the police? Turn to **2**.

Would you search the camp first, although it means delaying going to the police? Turn to **35**.

Would you go to Mr Silver, the camp security man? Turn to **56**.

Would you wait and see what happens next? Turn to **60**.

Detective Rating

Score 2 points if you knew straight away it was Porky and somebody else.

Score 1 point if you made one wrong choice in 13.

Score 2 extra points if you knew who it was straight away.

Deduct 1 point for each wrong alternative you chose in 82.

27

'Porky couldn't do it on his own,' said Casey. 'He had to have somebody to help him! Somebody who made sure we came to the part of the island where we would find the map.'

'Birdy Hamill,' said James.

'Birdy? But she was so nice . . .' My voice trailed away. I was remembering the conversation on the boat—Beans telling her all about us being the Mystery Squad and Birdy telling us about the Spanish Gold . . .

'She led us to the map!' I said, bitterly. 'With all those names. Blood Bay! Dagger Point! Spyglass Head! Deadman's Cove! Burial Mountain! Straight out of a silly kid's adventure story!'

'And we fell for it,' said Casey. 'We let her land us where she wanted to, and pick our camp site.'

'She showed me the best spot to get water from the stream!' I said.

'Where there just happened to be a treasure map that had been hidden for hundreds of years,' said Casey. 'One that hadn't been eroded by the small stones and water passing over it.'

'Which means that our so-called friend Birdy and the Divers are in this together,' said James. 'She must have found out what Mr Silver was up to, using us for secret surveillance on the island. She told the Devil Divers and together they worked out this treasure hunt scheme.'

'It's okay,' said Casey. 'Great, really.'

'What?'

'The scheme hasn't worked, has it?'

'EH?'

'Well . . . Birdy and the Devil Divers sent us off on a treasure hunt, right? We fell for it. They *saw* us falling for it . . . they must have had someone watching. They think we're out of the way.'

'And they think we're pretty stupid!' said Beans.

'That will *help* too,' said Casey. 'I mean, who would imagine that any kids stupid enough to fall for that treasure hunt story could cause any real trouble?'

'They've also given us one vital clue on a plate,' said James, suddenly.

'Right,' said Casey.

'We don't know what the Devil Divers are up to,' said James. 'But we certainly know where to look!'

Where would you look?

Look at the map in **74** to refresh your memory.

The Whistling Teeth rocks? Turn to **83**.

Spyglass Head? Turn to **20**.

Blood Bay? Turn to **43**.

Burial Mountain? Turn to **79**.

Deadman's Cove? Turn to **68**.

28

Wrong. Go to **52** and have another try.

29

Wrong. Move to **21**.

30

What would you expect to see if the car had moved recently? Look at the picture in **14**. Your destination is **39**.

31

Wrong. Go to **71**.

32

Porky is lying . . . but how did Casey know? If you know, turn to **14**.

If you need help turn to **11**.

33

Wrong. Turn to **47** and try again.

34

In a struggle, things get broken, like the clock. One thing, perhaps an accident. Two things? Can you find another breakage?

Your next stop is **47**.

35

Supposing Casey's dad hasn't been kidnapped, but he is investigating something . . . rushing around the camp asking questions will draw attention to what he is doing. Turn to **26** and think about another option.

36

Wrong. Go to **13** and reconsider.

37

Wrong. Go to **58** and think again.

38

Trying to rush a man you have reason to believe may be a violent criminal doesn't make sense. Two kids versus one crook equals ☆

Go to **59** and think again.

Detective Rating

If you noticed, the grass growing high around the car wheels you score 3 points.

2 points if you needed help.

Deduct 1 point if you thought Casey was right to begin with.

0 points if you didn't spot the grass.

39

'The grass around the wheels,' I said. 'The Devil Divers' car is heavily laden with all their equipment. If it had moved at all, it would have been bound to flatten the grass.'

'Well done, Bodge!' said James.

'It must have moved, to get there in the first place!' Beans objected.

'That's why Bodge said it must have been where it is for a long time,' said James.

'Oh,' said Beans.

'This isn't doing anything to get my dad back!' said Casey.

'Beans and I will keep an eye on the Devil Divers,' I said. 'You and James go and see Mr Silver . . . quickly.'

'I'll stay with Beans,' said James. 'You go with Casey, Bodger.'

'But . . .'

'One small one, one big one,' said James.

I made a face at Beans. James was being big brother again. He didn't trust the two of us on our own.

'Come on, Bodge,' said Casey. 'There's no time to lose.'

Mr Silver was in his hut when we got there . . . just about! He was so tall that his head looked as if it should be popping through the ceiling. He moved around inside with a permanent stoop making the small hut look as if it had been made for a garden gnome.

'What's up?' he said, looking down at us.

'Casey's dad has been kidnapped and those Devil Divers did it and old Porky . . . the fat one. . . he tried to fool us by saying that Casey's dad had a message to go back home and we know it isn't true because . . .'

'Hey, wait a minute,' said Silver, flopping down in a chair and wiggling his long legs in amusement. 'You're too quick for me, son.'

'Casey's dad was investigating something and now he's been kidnapped and we know who did it and Casey's dad was in a fight and we reckon . . .'

'Let me tell it, Bodger,' said Casey.

By the time he had finished Mr Silver didn't half look sick!

'Stay there, kids!' he ordered, and he rushed out of his hut to the camp office, where the telephone was. He had a funny loping run.

He was gone for a long time, and when he came back he made Casey go over it all again.

'I'll need this in writing for the police,' he said.

'Police?'

'Yeah. I've just been on to the top brass. Things are moving fast, I can tell you!'

'Great!' I said.

'Is there anything we can do to help?' Casey said.

He still sounded very shaken.

'You . . . no, nothing,' said Silver. 'These Devil Divers, whoever or whatever they are, have nabbed your dad. They'll be holding him somewhere. If they think we're on to them they might let him go. On the other hand, they might not.'

He paused, and let it sink in.

'This isn't a game for kids,' he said. 'The best thing you can do is to keep out of the way. The police will take over from now on. You won't see them, you won't hear them, but believe me every move those divers make will be watched. Look, kids, I know the way the police work. Sixteen years in the force. The most important thing is to get your father back, unhurt. Once that's done, there will be plenty of time to pick off this mob.'

Casey nodded.

'But I warn you,' said Silver. 'One false move by me, or you, or the police, and your dad could be in real trouble.'

'We've got their caravan under observation now,' I said.

'Have you?' said Silver.

'I don't think dad's there,' said Casey.

'I suppose it can't do any harm, so long as your friends don't give the game away,' said Silver.

'No chance!' I said. 'We're the Mys . . .'

'Shut up, Bodge,' said Casey. 'This is serious.'

'So is the Mystery Squad!' I said. 'We go around solving mysteries, and we're properly trained and everything! Keeping observation on people is one of the things we're trained to do.'

'Who trained you?'

'I did,' said Casey.

'Chip off the old block,' said Silver, 'I suppose
your dad has given you a few hints?'

'We've solved lots and lots of cases . . .' I said.

'I'm sure you have!' Silver said, giving us a What-
funny-little-kids look.

'Bodger's right, Mr Silver,' Casey said, and he
quickly outlined some of the things we'd done to help
Casey's dad. I could see that Silver was really
impressed.

'If there's anything we can do, anything at all,
we'd like to do it, Mr Silver,' I said, when Casey had
finished.

'You're just kids . . .' said Silver.

'We do have one advantage over you, and the
police,' said Casey, slowly.

'What's that?'

'The Devil Divers are used to seeing us around the
camp. If the police start to follow them, they may
notice something. They won't notice us.'

'They won't see us, we're good at observation!'
I said.

'They won't *notice* us, even if they do see us,
Bodger,' said Casey. 'That's the whole point. They
expect us to be about the place.'

'You've got something there,' Silver said. 'You say
you've done this sort of thing before . . . ?'

'Not officially,' said Casey.

'Sure, of course not. But . . . wait, I'll have to put
in another call to H.Q. They won't like using kids,
but just the same . . .'

Mr Silver was gone for a good fifteen minutes this
time.

'I bet they say no,' said Casey.

'We could do it anyway,' I said.

'Give over, Bodge!' said Casey. 'This time, we do what we're told.'

Silver came back, looking even grimmer than before.

'I spoke to the top brass,' he said. 'They don't like it. So, sorry, no surveillance round the camp.'

Our faces fell.

'However, surveillance round the camp is one thing. It's easy enough to slip a few policemen in here without being noticed, but surveillance at their base on Whistling Island is quite another.'

'On Whistling Island?' gasped Casey. I don't know if he was thinking what I was thinking, but I wasn't too keen. Whistling Island is an odd place, with funny rock formations and caves on it. The wind whistles through them . . . that's where it got its name. It's a bit spooky, if you ask me.

'The Devil Divers are supposed to be working round the Whistling Teeth, those sharp rocks by the end of the island. They have a base somewhere near the bay. I pointed out that it would be almost impossible to land a party of police there to check things out without being noticed . . . but a group of kids, camping . . . you could check the caves, see what they are up to . . .'

'Y-e-s,' said Casey, doubtfully.

'But no heroics, eh? Absolutely no risks taken. All you do is to go to the island, have a look round, check the caves, and try to pick up any clues you might find as to what they're really doing . . .'

'They're diving.'

'If they're only diving, they're hardly going to concern themselves with your dad, young Casey,' said Silver. 'There's more to it than that.'

'Right,' said Casey.

'You go to the island, light a bonfire, have a picnic, have a swim, do whatever else kids do these days . . . you keep your eyes open and, most important of all, you keep out of trouble. Okay? Absolutely no risks.'

I didn't like the sound of that.

'No risks, and not a word to a soul. Right?' said Silver. 'I'll find someone to take you out to the island . . .'

'We've got tents,' I said.

'Great,' said Silver. 'Make a night of it then. The darkness will give you cover. But no tricks, do you understand? I'm risking my reputation on this, and so is Jack Bradley at H.Q. Using kids on a real case, where there's danger . . . if it wasn't your dad, Casey . . . well, I don't know.'

He sounded as if he was having second thoughts.

'It is my dad, Mr Silver,' said Casey. 'He's in danger, and I'm going through with this to help him!'

'What about you?' Silver said, turning his attention to me. 'Scared?'

'Nope!' I said.

'Good boy!' he laughed, and then he grew serious again. 'Remember, whatever else you do, absolute secrecy is vital.'

We went back to the caravan without a word, knowing that we were involved in the most important case the Mystery Squad had ever had to tackle.

'Does absolute secrecy mean we can't tell Beans and James, Casey?' I asked.

''Course not,' he said. 'One for all, all for one.'

Casey was trying to sound brave about it, but I don't think either of us felt brave.

Beans and James weren't at the caravan, but they had left a code message telling us where they were and what they were doing.

Can you read the code message?

If you can break the code turn to **59**.

If you need help turn to **63**.

40

Two kids against one grown man . . . particularly a crook who isn't afraid of being violent means someone will get badly hurt . . . probably you! Think again, go to **59**.

41

Wrong. Go to **13** and reconsider.

42

READ ANY GOOD BOOKS LATELY? That's your clue. Turn to **26**.

43

Wrong! Go to **27** and think again.

44

Too small.
Too tall.
Get it?
Got it?
Good.

Go to **73** and consider the alternatives.

45

Wrong! Move on to **51**.

Detective Rating

4 points here! Deduct 1 for each custard pie you collected in the last section.

46

'Lobster pots!' I said. 'There aren't any lobsters here, remember Casey told us? Pollution from the Power Station killed them off. But there are lobster *pots* . . . filled with *what*?'

We didn't have time to think about it, because at that moment Birdy and the Divers appeared. They were carrying some of the lobster pots.

Birdy spotted James and Casey!

'Hey! Hey you!' she shouted.

Casey looked up, and tugged James' sleeve. They didn't hang about on board the Divers' boat. James picked something up and threw it over the side, and the next minute the two of them were in the water, heading for the *Morning Dew*.

So were the others.

It was no contest. James and Casey beat them by a long way. Birdy and old fat Porky were still scrambling round the side of the bay when James and Casey climbed dripping on board.

'Get going, Bodge!' gasped Casey.

'I don't know how to start her . . .'

James pushed past me and reached for the controls. The next moment the engine roared into life. I grabbed the wheel, and we were off, heading round the Whistling Teeth in a fountain of spray.

I've never gone so fast in a boat in my life. It was really great! We had beaten them and we were getting away and . . .

Something went wrong!

There was a terrible jolt, the boat jerked almost to a stop, then the front bucked wildly with the engine churning. The next minute we were free of whatever had been stopping us but we were out of control and heading full speed for the Whistling Teeth.

'Bodge!' Beans shouted.
We crashed right into the rocks!

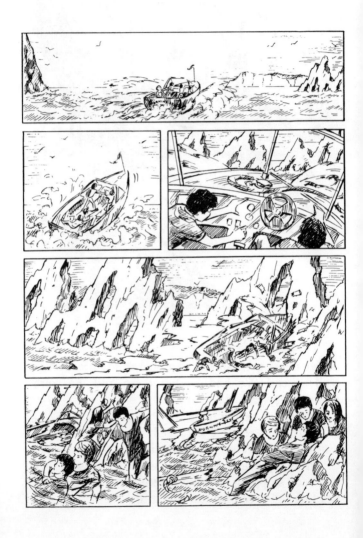

I don't know what happened next. I remember being in the water, and I remember Casey getting hold of me from behind.

Next thing I was lying on a rock with my legs still in the water and I heard Beans saying 'He's dead! Old Bodge is dead.'

'He's not,' said Casey.

I didn't say anything. I was too dazed to speak.

'Lie still, Bodge,' Casey said.

I lay where I was till I remembered how I'd got there, and what was happening.

'Casey!' I said, sitting up.

'Shut up and sit still, Bodge,' said Casey.

'The Divers . . .'

'They can't get at us and we can't get at them, Bodge,' said James.

'What are we going to do?'

We all looked at Casey.

'Signal!' he said. Trust Casey to think of something to do! 'Signal to the mainland for help.'

'How?' I said.

'You're the "How" man, James,' said Casey.

'Semaphore,' said James. 'We take off our shirts and use them as flags, to signal in semaphore.'

'We wouldn't be seen,' said Casey. 'Kids on a rock waving shirts about . . . we haven't even got red ones.'

'We can use timber from the boat,' said James. 'Fish some of it up . . . or an oar, if you can lay hands on one. We can make great big arms for the semaphore.'

That's what we did. James and Casey got an oar and a long broken plank, and fixed a shirt to each of them, giving us two semaphore planks. Then James climbed to the highest point on our rock and began signalling to the shore.

We decided to send this message: HELP. SEND POLICE. PETERS. We put PETERS at the end because we reckoned the police would recognise the name.

Can you send the message?

Write out the Mystery Squad's message in semaphore, then turn to **69**.

Detective Rating

3 points if you found the broken pipe straight away.
2 points if you needed help.

47

'Dad's pipe,' said Casey. 'Or what's left of it! It's really smashed.'

He picked up the pieces of the pipe from under the table, where he'd spotted them.

'Some sort of struggle,' he said. 'Dad's pipe gets broken, and the travelling clock, then . . .' He broke off, shrugging his shoulders. 'What then?'

'Depends who won, doesn't it?' James said. 'I mean if you're saying someone came in and ambushed your dad, then anything could have happened.'

'I bet he's been kidnapped and held to ransom for millions!' I said.

'I don't think we've got millions,' said Casey.

'Then your dad will be cut up in little bits and fed to the lobsters!' I said.

Nobody smiled.

'It's serious, Bodger,' James said.

'Yes, shut up, Bodge,' said Beans.

'Anyway, there are no lobsters round here,' Casey said. 'Mr Carne down at the harbour said it was something to do with discharges from the Power Station.'

Nobody said anything.

'I expect he'll turn up in a minute,' Beans broke the silence.

'Suppose he doesn't, though?' said Casey.

'Kidnapped . . .'

'Shut up, Bodge!'

'Bodge could be right,' Casey said, uneasily. 'A lot of people have it in for my dad because he's a policeman. What if some of them tried to get at him when he was off guard, on holiday?'

'Wait a minute,' said James. 'This could be a lot of fuss about nothing. All we've got is a broken pipe and a broken travelling clock. That's not much to go on. Perhaps he tripped and fell, knocking the clock off the table and breaking his pipe at the same time. No fight. No kidnappers!'

There was a pause while we thought about it.

'Who did the tidying up?' said Casey.

'Your dad did,' said James.

'Not likely,' said Casey.

'A lot more likely than his being kidnapped,' said James.

'I bet he'll be back in a minute,' said Beans. 'I bet he went off to the shop to get a new pipe! That's what he did! That explains it. Busting his pipe and needing a new one is an emergency as far as your dad's concerned.' She tried to make a joke of it to cheer us up.

'The camp shop hasn't got pipes,' I said. 'He'd have to go into town . . . which explains why he's so late!'

'I hope you're right,' said Casey, who was still looking a bit green.

'I might be able to prove it!' I said, suddenly remembering.

'How?' said Casey.

'I thought your dad was up to something and I kind of . . . sort of . . .'

'You *didn't*!' said Beans. 'That's rotten, Bodger.'

'It's *meant* for surveillance of suspects, not people like Casey's dad!' said James, as I switched on.

Switched on what?

Check the picture in **47**.

If you think it was the lamp, turn to **76**.

If you think it was the clock, turn to **33**.

If you think it was something else, turn to **65**.

48

You've been custard pied. Go to **27** and think again.

49

Think again! Turn to **60** and consider the alternatives.

50

Right!
But why had they no reason to be there?
Now turn to **46**.

51

You've got a black spot on your record
That's a clue. Go to **15**.
Or take another clue before you go, by turning to **3**.

Detective Rating

If you realised what the dew would do to the cigar ash take 3 points.

If you needed a clue, take 2!

52

'Dew!' said Beans. 'The morning dew!'

'What?'

'Beans is right, Bodger,' said James. 'Dew would have wet the cigar butt and destroyed the powdery ash on the end.'

'Which means the cigar butt was dropped here today, well after dawn,' said Beans.

'Which means the Divers were here, or at least Porky was . . .'

'And possibly my dad!' said Casey, biting his lip.

'Hidden on the island somewhere? You think they ran him out on their boat?'

'If he's hidden here, then we'll find him!' I said. 'Probably we'll find the Spanish Gold as well, and solve the Secret of the Whistling Teeth.'

Casey shrugged. He wasn't much interested in the treasure, just his dad.

'Come on,' said James. 'Time we moved camp.'

'Where to?'

'We want to be able to see this spot. Maybe the Divers will come back.'

We started packing up our stuff.

'Better take some water with us,' James suggested. 'Bodger, you can be water carrier!'

I took the billycan down to the place Birdy had shown us and dipped it in. Then I saw IT. It was *almost* the most exciting discovery I have ever made in my whole life, or at least I thought it was then, but *then* I didn't know what was coming next.

'Casey! James!' I shouted. They all came running and bent down beside me while I lifted out the stone. 'It's a map . . . a hidden map, scratched on this stone. I found it in the water . . . it must have been there for years and years. It's the wreckers' map!'

Casey took it from me.

'The island?' he said, showing it to James.

James studied it. 'It *could* be,' he said.

'That first word is IN,' said Beans. 'Look . . . a bit of the I has gone and part of the N but it is definitely IN.'

'And THE, that's clear.'

'IN THE SKULLS,' said James, working at the stone with his hands to clear away the grime. It was all scratchy, but definitely a Treasure Map.

'What's that letter?' I said. 'Is it meant to be an O?'

'It's the picture of an eye,' said Casey. 'And the message means IN THE SKULL'S EYE.'

'The Treasure is in the Skull's Eye!' I gasped. 'Up there . . . the Skull Rock . . . I bet we've found the Treasure! All because I was sharp-eyed and spotted this old stone! I bet it's been hidden for trillions of years in the river bed and now I've come along and spotted it and . . . SPANISH GOLD!'

'What do we do?' said James, doubtfully. 'We're supposed to be looking for Casey's dad . . .'

'He might be there too!' I said. 'Supposing the Devil Divers are looking for the treasure and they know there are caves up there in the Skull Rock . . .'

'They'd search the caves . . .' said Beans.

'And make their camp here while they were doing it. And then if they had to put Casey's dad somewhere that would be a brilliant place to put him.'

'Are there caves?' said Casey.

'Let's go and find out!'

There were lots of caves. The Skull Rock was riddled with them—small, dark holes leading back into the soft stone.

'You could search here for ever and not find the right one,' said Casey, gloomily.

'In the Skull's Eye,' I said, 'we know the right one!'

We climbed up the face of the Skull.

'Don't look down,' James warned us.

Nobody wanted to. It was old rock, very soft and crumbly, and we were afraid it would give way beneath us.

We worked our way round the bit like a nose, and up to the nearest eye.

'The Skull's Eye!' I breathed.

'Looks like a cave to me,' said Beans, and off she darted into it. 'A treasure cave!'

'Wait!' shouted Casey, but Beans was gone. We had to go after her.

'Got your torch?' said James. I pulled my torch out and flicked it on. A good detective always comes equipped for emergencies.

It was dark in the cave but the air was fresh and we could move quite easily, to begin with at any rate.

'Steps?' I said, flashing my torch down.

'Could be, could be rock formation,' said James.

We started going down, then the floor evened out again. We caught up with Beans.

'Rock fall,' she said. 'The way's blocked.'

There was a trickle of water down the fallen rock. It had eaten a path into the stone.

'Well?' said James. 'What do we do?'

'Burrow through!' I said. 'The treasure must be hidden on the other side. Perhaps this was one of

those trap tunnels. You went in after the treasure
without knowing the secret and the tunnel collapsed
on you and killed you.'

'This tunnel collapsed a long time ago,' said
James. 'You can tell from the way that trickling
water has cut into the stone.'

'The treasure has been hidden a long time,' I pointed out. 'Let's try and dislodge some of those stones and work our way through to the other side. I bet we'll find the Treasure Room where the Spanish Gold is hidden.'

'If it isn't in the other eye!' said James suddenly.

That stopped us. We hadn't thought of that.

'Or . . . or hidden in the wall of the tunnel, some-where?' I suggested. 'Perhaps there is a sort of . . . sort of safe thing, only not a safe, but you know what I mean.'

'Or another clue? Another clue scratched on a stone? The stone could be in the wall somewhere, and we've got to find it!' Beans said.

'Like a kid's adventure story,' said Casey, 'The Secret of the Spanish Gold.'

Have you solved The Secret of the Spanish Gold?

If you think there's a secret safe in the wall of the tunnel, turn to **12**.

If you think there's a hidden clue to its where-abouts scratched on the wall, turn to **24**.

If you think it's hidden in the other eye, turn to **66**.

If you think there's a Treasure Room further down the tunnel beyond the dislodged stones, turn to **28**.

If you think it's just a kid's adventure story, turn to **13**.

53

Wrong choice. Turn to **74** and try again.

54

You're right . . . how did they plan to do it?
Your next destination is **73**.

55

Wrong. Turn to **82** and try again.

56

Casey's dad is only half an hour late. If he is working undercover on another case, he wouldn't want his cover blown, would he? Turn to **26** and consider the other options.

57

Wrong! Move on to **51**.

Detective Rating

3 points if you got the whole message right.
2 points for just one mistake.

58

```
- . - . -          BEGIN
                   MESSAGE
. - -              W
                   E
.                  A
. -                R
. - .              E
.                  A
. - . .            L
                   R
. -                E
.                  A
. -                D
- . .              Y
- . - -            O
- - -              N
- . - -            O
. - . .            U
. - .              R
. - -              W
. -                A
- . - -            Y
. - . - .          END
                   MESSAGE
```

'Great!' said James.

'Rescue!' said Beans.

'Not so great,' said Casey. 'The signal is coming from the ruined tower, right? We've been signalling to the enemy! Remember the telescope? WATCHING DIVERS AT RUINED TOWER.'

'We were watching Porky,' said James. 'Then a man came up, and chased him off!'

'What?' said Casey.

They didn't have time to argue about it, for at that

moment we heard the throb of an engine. And not just one engine . . . lots of them. Round the far side of the cove came three police patrol boats . . . very fast!

'Rescue!' I said, sitting up.

And it was.

The police arrested Birdy, Porky and the divers together with their lobster pots. The men in the boat that picked us up looked pleased as punch . . . but not so pleased as Casey looked when the fourth boat arrived. In it was his dad. With him was the man who had chased us from the ruined tower.

'Commander Burton, Special Operations,' said Casey's dad. 'This is my son Casey, and his friends . . . the Mystery Squad of whom you've heard so much.'

The man shook our hands.

'Well done,' he said. 'We were worried about you. Your dad was being held by John Silver, the so-called security officer at the camp, but he managed to break free. We got Silver . . . then found we'd lost you!'

'All's well that ends well,' said Casey's dad. 'Though I nearly put my foot in it and mucked up your operation, Commander!'

'We had the island under special surveillance,' explained Commander Burton. 'We were waiting to pick off Silver and his friends as soon as they tried to move the bullion.'

'Bullion?' I gasped. '*Gold* bullion?'

'The result of the big South African bullion job last year,' said Commander Burton. 'We were tipped off that Silver had the stuff hidden somewhere. We decided to let him find it for us . . . which he almost did.'

'Almost?'

'Some of the bullion is missing,' said Commander Burton.

I looked at Casey. A big idea was beginning to form in my mind.

'We caught them red-handed with the stuff in the lobster-pots,' said Commander Burton. 'Clever, that! All stowed underwater, with just a few surface buoys to mark the spot.'

'Then the divers *were* diving . . .' said Beans, in a puzzled voice.

'Porky Phillips dive?' laughed the Commander. 'No! All they had to do was grapple the ropes and draw the stuff in. We were waiting to see how they proposed to get it clear of the island . . . a bit at a time, probably, using the two boats . . . though even that would be a risky operation. You could bring in a small bag or two at a time, but any large amount of gold bullion would be noticed.'

'Bodger sank one of the boats,' said James. 'The *Morning Dew.*'

'Bodger can't steer for nuts!' said Beans. 'He drove right into the rocks and almost killed us!'

'Lay off him, Beans!' said James.

'He looks a bit pale, doesn't he?' said Commander Burton. 'You feel all right, son?'

'I know where the rest of the bullion is,' I said.

'Eh?' Commander Burton blinked at me.

'He thinks it's up in the Skull's Eye Cave!' said Beans, scornfully.

'No I don't,' I said. 'I've worked out how the Devil Divers planned to move the bullion, without it being seen on board the two boats, and that tells me roughly where it is now!'

How were the Devil Divers going to move the bullion?

By hiding it in the CO^2 cylinders? Turn to **5**.

By swimming in with it at night? Turn to **37**.

By towing it in the fishing nets? Turn to **19**.

Detective Rating

WATCHING DIVERS AT RUINED TOWER
BEANS AND JAMES

4 points if you decoded the message without help.

3 points if you solved it with help.

Deduct 1 point for each square you got wrong, or failed to solve.

59

It didn't take us long to work out the code message.

'WATCHING,' said Casey. 'That's the first word. The next one is DIVERS—that's dead easy. Then CAT minus C.'

'That's AT,' I said, 'but it's a rotten drawing.'

'I don't get this one,' said Casey. 'Looks like a house that's been knocked about a bit, plus ED. What does that mean?'

'HOUSE-ED?' I said. 'No . . . WATCHING DIVERS AT HOUSED wouldn't make sense.'

'Another rotten drawing!' said Casey. 'If that's meant to be a house it's all in ruins!'

'RUIN!' I said. 'That's it. RUIN and ED that gives us RUINED.'

'The next one's a flower, minus FL gives OWER and plus T gives TOWER!' said Casey. 'That would make the final message: WATCHING DIVERS AT RUINED TOWER BEANS AND JAMES.'

'Good old James!' I said.

It was really a smart move to use the top of the tower for watching the divers. Beans and James could see without being seen, which was exactly what they needed to do.

We went to the tower.

No sign of life.

There was a rough wire gate across the entrance. We pushed through it and went up the steps on to the top.

'Look at that!' said Casey.

'It's a telescope. I've seen one like it in James's book!' I said.

'And it's trained on Whistling Island,' said Casey, taking a squint through the viewwinder. 'On the rocks, the Whistling Teeth.'

'The police . . . ?' I said. Then I realised that it couldn't be the police, they wouldn't have had time to set up the operation.

'Where the Devil Divers are supposed to be diving,' said Casey.

'But . . .'

I didn't get any further, because at that moment we heard the wire gate at the foot of the tower scrape as someone came through it and started up the stairs.

'STAY WHERE YOU ARE!' someone shouted.

We were trapped.

Trapped? What would you do?

Would you stay where you are and try to talk your way out of trouble? Turn to **16**.

Would you try to take the newcomer prisoner by ambushing him as he reaches the top of the stairs? Turn to **40**.

Would you attempt to escape by rushing past the man down the stairs? Turn to **38**.

Would you risk a broken leg by jumping off the tower? Turn to **4**.

Would you shout for help and hope for the best? Turn to **75**.

Detective Rating

4 points if you got the right answer straight away.
Deduct 1 for each wrong choice you made.

60

'On the basis of the evidence so far, we do nothing!'
said James. 'We wait and see what happens.'

'*Nothing*?' Casey protested. He was worried sick
about his dad, anybody could see that.

'We've got to do *something*,' said Beans.

'You're not thinking!' said James. 'We've only got
one firm bit of evidence, and that is that Casey's dad
isn't here. The clock and the pipe suggest that there
could have been a struggle and something *could* have
happened to him . . .'

'Kidnapped!' I said.

'Or he could have tripped, knocked the clock over,
broken his pipe, and gone to get another one! That's
one explanation. There could be lots of others!'
others!'

'We still ought to be doing something,' Beans
insisted.

'He's my dad!' said Casey. 'If he's in trouble . . .'

'We know he had spotted something crooked
going on, right? He wanted a chance to investigate it
quietly, with us out of the way. So . . . that's what
he's doing. If we start rushing round the camp telling
people Casey's dad is a policeman and he's been
kidnapped . . .?'

'We blow Dad's cover,' said Casey, reluctantly.

'All because he's half an hour late back to the caravan.'

'Forty minutes,' I said.

'If Dad is investigating something, the last thing he'd want is for us to start a fuss by saying he's been kidnapped,' Casey admitted.

'He'd expect us to weigh up the evidence, and wait until we had good grounds to act . . . not go dashing off because Bodger has started dreaming up kidnappers and ransoms!' said James.

'I never!' I said. 'I only thought it *might* be.'

'You did,' said Beans. 'The trouble with you, Bodge, is that you've got too much imagination for an investigator!'

'Shut up, you two,' said Casey.

'Agreed then? We do nothing, at least for another hour or two, by which time your dad will probably have turned up. If he hasn't, then that's more evidence . . . and it justifies our doing something. Even your dad couldn't complain about that. It would be the only sensible thing to do.'

'*Hey. You kids!*'

We spun round at the sound of the strange voice. It was the porky guy from the Devil Divers, and he was standing at the open door puffing at a fat cigar. He'd been listening to every word we said.

'You kids!' he said. 'I got a message for one of you, young Peters.'

'That's me,' said Casey.

'Right. Your dad had to hop back to town. Got a phone message from your mum. A bit of bother— said to tell you nothing serious.'

'Did he?' said Casey.

'Yeh. He reckoned he'd spend the night there. Be back some time tomorrow. He left you this, for chips and stuff. Okay?'

Old Porky put some money on the table.

'Your dad asked us to keep an eye out for you,' he said. 'So anything you need, come down to the van, and me or one of the boys will sort it out for you. Savvy?'

'Thanks very much,' said Casey.

'No problems?'

'No problems,' said Casey.

'Right! See you, then! Don't do anything I wouldn't do, will you?'

Off he went.
Casey turned to us, looking pale.

Why is Casey looking pale?
He's worried about the 'bit of bother'? Turn to **25**.
Porky's lying? Turn to **32**.
Some other reason? Turn to **49**.

Detective Rating

3 points for getting here but *you lose 1 point for each other option you chose first.*

61

'Long John *Silver*,' said Casey. 'Out of the book *Treasure Island*. It's like one of Dad's jokes. Long John Silver and his Parrot . . . our Mr Silver, and *his* Birdy!'

'Oh,' said James.

'We knew that Dad had been talking to Silver, and we reckoned he must be all right, because he was the camp security man . . .'

'He was a policeman,' I said. 'He worked with your dad.'

'That's what *he* said,' said Casey. 'Doesn't mean it's true.'

'He sent us out here, well away from any help, and got Birdy to put us right off the track with her treasure story,' said James.

'I don't know what I was thinking of!' said Casey. 'I should have known the police wouldn't send us on surveillance . . . they just don't use kids like that . . . not even us!' he added, when he saw I was about to protest.

'You mean Silver's a crook?' I said.

'And Dad was investigating him! That's what this note means. "L.J. and Parrot? Treasure Island?!" Dad knew Silver was a crook and he knew that something was going on at the island. He was waiting for Birdy to show up . . . Birdy and Silver must work together.'

'And now they've got your dad . . . and they've got us well out of the way, where we can't raise the alarm!' said James. 'It doesn't even matter much if we spot what they're doing . . . they've got us trapped!'

'That's what they think,' said Casey. 'But they're wrong!'

I brightened up. I was pretty sure Casey had a plan.

I was right.

'We're on an island,' said Casey. 'There's only one way to get off it, right?'

'Right,' I said. 'By boat.'

'And there are two boats,' said James, looking up. 'The one belonging to the Divers, and the one belonging to Birdy, the *Morning Dew*.'

'We turn the trap round . . . we trap them!' said Casey. 'We put their boat out of action and steal the other one! We head for the shore and get help.'

'Great!' I said.

'Fine,' said James.

Neither of us said anything about Casey's dad. It was a grand scheme, but it put him in even more danger.

'Bodger, stick on Beans's cap!' said Casey. 'James and I are going to "help" poor little "Beans" get down to the *Morning Dew*. Just in case they're still watching us!'

I never thought I'd be dressing up as Beans!

We started off over North Point, following the stream past Skull Rock. There was no sign of Beans until we were almost at Deadman's Cove, and then something rattled on the rocks beside us.

A stone.

'Where is she?' asked James.

Beans popped up out of the heather, almost at our feet.

'It's all right,' she said. 'There's nobody watching. They're all down on the rocks moving some heavy stuff. I can't see what it is.'

Quickly, Casey explained our plan to Beans.

'Is Birdy with the men?' he asked.

Beans nodded.

'Right!' said Casey. 'You two go down to the *Morning Dew* and get ready to move off, fast! James and I have to pay a visit to the Divers' boat.'

The *Morning Dew* was moored fairly close into the shore . . . it's a good thing it was, because my swimming isn't too hot.

'Okay?' Beans said.

'Yeh,' I said, inspecting the controls. I'd steered the boat once, but I wasn't certain how to start her.

'Keep down,' said Beans. 'We don't want to be spotted.'

We crouched in the boat, peering across at the Divers' boat.

'Hey!' I said, suddenly. 'I bet those are a clue!'

'What?'

I ignored Beans. 'There's no reason for them to be here . . . unless something was hidden in them . . . where no one would be likely to notice . . .'

What's Bodger talking about?
The lobster pots? Turn to **50**.
The cylinders? Turn to **9**.
The buoys? Turn to **29**.
The planks? Turn to **67**.

Detective Rating

If you discovered the butt by the stone score 3 points.
Deduct 1 point for each wrong choice you made.
0 points if you didn't find the butt.

62

'One of Porky's cigar butts,' said Casey, picking it up. The powdery ash flicked off the end. 'Which shows our famous cigar-smoking Devil Diver has been here . . . today.'

'Why today?' said Beans, and then her face cleared. 'Oh! I see. It's been dry today, hasn't it?'

'Right!' said Casey.

'It was dry yesterday, too,' I objected.

How did Casey and Beans know that Porky had been there that day?

If you know the answer turn to **52**.

If you need a clue turn to **17**.

63

This is a picture of a watch, plus 'ing.'

WATCH + ING = Watching.

That's the first work in the message.

Solved the rest? Turn to **59**. Need another look? Go back to **39**.

64

Wrong! Turn to **82** and try again.

65

You're right . . . it was a miniature tape recorder rigged by James for Mystery Squad operations. Now go to **47** and find it!

If you think you've found it, turn to **26**.

If you need help turn to **42**.

66

Wrong. Go to **52** and have another try.

67

Wrong. Move to **21**.

68

Right. How did James know? Your next stop is **71**.

Detective Rating

You score 3 points if you got the whole message right.
You score 2 points if you made only one mistake.

69

H E L P   S E N D

P O L I C E   P E T E R S

James and Casey sent our message again and again and again.

We began to think nobody would ever spot us.
Then a light blinked . . . from the ruined tower!

Here is the basic Morse Code!

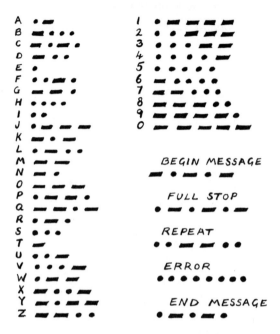

Decode the message.

Turn to **58** when you've finished.

Detective Rating

4 points if you spotted the short drop!
Deduct 1 point for each wrong choice you made.

70

'Jump, Bodge,' Casey said.

I gaped at him. 'We'll break our necks!' I said.

'Not *that* side,' said Casey.

He was right! There was only a short drop on the other side, with a cushion of bracken to land on.

'Hey! Hey you, come back!' the man shouted, but we weren't coming back!

'That was too close for comfort!' Casey panted, when we got down to the beach.

'What went wrong?' I gasped. 'Where are they?'

'I don't know,' said Casey. 'Maybe that man caught them.'

'Maybe we decoded the message wrong,' I said.

'Or decoded it correctly, but didn't understand what it meant!' said Casey.

What do you think?

James and Beans have been captured at the tower?
Turn to **78**.

Casey and Bodger decoded the message incorrectly?
Turn to **7**.

They decoded correctly, but made a mistake about
what it meant? Turn to **23**.

Detective Rating

Birdy invented a story to keep them away from Deadman's Cove. 4 points if you worked it out straight away. Deduct 1 point for each wrong choice you made. You score 1 point if you picked Deadman's Cove first time, but were unable to work out why.

71

'Birdy dreamed up the treasure hunt to keep us out of the way,' said Casey. 'We almost fell for it. Then she spoiled things. She told us where she *didn't* want us to go.'

'Huh?'

'The other part of the kid's story—about dead wreckers in Deadman's Cove. All those whistling ghosts! She reckoned we'd be terrified to go there after dusk and even if we did risk it and heard something, we'd think it was the ghosts!'

'But now we know exactly where to start investigating,' said James.

'What about the Whistling Teeth?' I said. 'She warned us off those as well.'

'The Whistling Teeth are a cover story,' said James. 'Whatever our friends are up to, they're not too keen on diving, that's for sure.'

'But . . . but . . . all that equipment?'

'They're not divers,' Casey broke in. 'I thought you knew that. James and I realised that ages ago, at the caravan. Call yourself a member of the Mystery Squad . . .'

Beans tried to look as if she had known about the divers all along, which is just like her.

'*How* do you know they're not real divers?' I said.
'They look professional enough to me!'

'Professional divers?' said James. 'Do leave off,
Bodge.'

'CO_2!' said Casey. 'Carbon dioxide! You'd have a
chilly old pair of lungs if you tried diving with tanks
of that strapped to your back as an air supply!'

'What?'

'The air tanks they had at the caravan were marked
CO_2. That would kill a diver. But their equipment
was the real give-away. Deep sea divers have to take
great care of their equipment. Our friends the Devil
Divers left it all heaped up in the back of their estate
car, like a load of old rubbish.'

'If they're not divers, what are they doing?' I
asked.

Casey shrugged.

'Process of deduction,' said James. 'Either they're hiding something on the island, or taking something off it! All those boat trips back and forwards.'

'What sort of something?' I asked.

Nobody knew.

'Well, we won't find out by standing here!' said Casey.

'Wait,' said James. 'Process of deduction again! They bothered to lay a false trail to send us on a treasure hunt, wanting us out of the way. Don't you think they'll have someone checking that we've followed it?'

'Y-e-s,' said Casey slowly.

'In other words, the entrance to the cave is being watched. They'll have seen us going in and somebody will be waiting for us to come out again.'

'Couldn't we give the watcher the slip?' I said.

'Stay in here until dark, then try to slip out. Or try to lure the watcher into a trap,' said Casey.

'Like an elephant trap?' I said.

'Yes. Or three of us could make a diversion while one gets away.'

We discussed the three options, and decided on a plan.

'Right,' said Casey. 'First step is for someone to go back to the camp and pick up what we need.' He made out a list:

> 2 tent poles
> tent canvas
> 2 kit bags
> 1 blanket
> 1 spare pair of Beans's socks
> several old hankies.

'What about the stones?' I said.

'They're all around us,' said Casey.

What is the plan?

Stay in the cave until dark and then slip out? Turn to **31**.

Try to lure the watcher into an elephant trap? Turn to **8**.

Make a diversion, so that one member of the party can escape? Turn to **54**.

Detective Rating

5 points for working out that the boat crashed because the bullion was secured in the net beneath it. Deduct 1 point for each wrong option selected.

72

We had a special slap-up dinner back at the caravan to celebrate me being the Best Detective in the World.

'Who worked out that the rest of the bullion was in a fishing net, attached to the bottom of the *Morning Dew*?' I said. 'You were on board too, remember. You know what it felt like. We started off too fast, the rope hawser tightened, held, and snapped, throwing us on to the rocks! If we had started off normally we'd have been able to drag the net along behind us, with the bullion bars in it.'

'Okay, so you're clever!' said James.

'He is clever!' said Casey's dad.

'Your best ever bit of detection, Bodge,' said Casey.

'Well done, Bodge!' said James.

'Big Head!' said Beans.

I took no notice of Beans. I was too busy sneaking the last of her sausages.

Now look at the Detective Rating Chart on page 95 and find out how good a detective you are!

Detective Rating

If you worked out that the plan was to make a dummy on a stretcher score 5 points. Deduct 1 point for each wrong choice. No points if you didn't work out what the plan was.

73

'Why does the dummy on the stretcher have to be Beans?' I objected.

'Because of her rotten hat,' said James. 'Anybody else on the stretcher and we've got to make the head

look convincing. This way, all that can be seen from a distance is the hat and the stuffed socks at the far end. It means Beans can wait until we've cleared off, taking whoever is watching us with us, and then she can sneak out unobserved and have a good look round while we take our "Fifth Man" back to the camp.'

'I would be better,' I said.

'Why would you be better?'

'He thinks he'd be better because he's a boy!' said Beans. 'Everybody knows I'm the best one at tracking without being spotted.'

'You're not!' I said. 'I'm the best tracker!'

'Shut up, Bodge,' said James. 'We have to make the dummy look like Beans, because we have to have the hat on it, right?'

'I could change clothes with her so that she looked like me!' I said.

'I'm not wearing your rotten clothes,' said Beans. 'You needn't think I am.'

'We're not leaving Bodge,' said James, firmly. 'You can forget that idea. It would be different if Casey or I could do it . . .'

'Why not?' said Casey. 'We dress the dummy as Beans, I stay behind in the cave, and you three carry the stretcher down to the camp?'

Would it work if Casey stays behind in Beans's place?

Yes? Turn to 22.

No? Turn to 80.

Need a clue? Turn to 44.

Detective Rating

James and Beans were watching the divers who were at the tower.

If you got it without making any wrong choices, 3 points.

One wrong choice, 2 points.

Two wrong choices, 1 point.

If you didn't get it, 0 points.

74

'The message didn't mean that James and Beans were at the tower, watching the divers . . . it meant that they were watching the divers who were AT the tower! And we walked straight into one of them!'

'Bodger . . . Casey!' Beans's voice interrupted us. She was coming across the beach toward us, with James and a woman we hadn't seen before.

'I'm Birdy Hamill,' the woman said. 'Mr Silver told me you kids were on the look-out for a boat to

take you across to Whistling Island. Going camping?'

'Er . . . yes,' said Casey.

'First I've heard of it,' muttered James, raising an eyebrow.

'It's okay, James,' said Casey.

'Well, get your stuff, and I'll run you over,' she said. 'That's my boat, the *Morning Dew*.'

It was a super boat, really fast, with lots of room for all our stuff. We piled in. James and Casey went to the back and had a talk, and meanwhile Birdy let me have a go at steering.

It was great! I felt like James Bond swishing across the water. It would have been even greater if we hadn't been worried about Casey's dad.

'Careful,' Birdy warned. 'Steer well clear of the Teeth . . . or they'll bite the bottom out of the boat!'

'I bet there's been loads of wrecks there,' said Beans, trying to sound casual. I knew what she was doing. She was pumping Birdy, to find out if there was anything the Divers might be diving for.

'There was a famous ship,' said Birdy slowly.

'A treasure ship?'

'So they say. The *Mary Estelle*. She was lured on to the Teeth by wreckers. Only one man escaped, and he swam to the mainland and raised the alarm. The wreckers were killed in a bloody fight in the cove but the treasure was never found. Either it sank with the ship, or the wreckers got it off and hid it in one of the caves on the island.'

'What sort of treasure?' Beans said. We were really on to something! It was like a book—sailing out to Treasure Island where hoards of gold and jewels lay hidden.

'Spanish Gold!' said Birdy.

'The Buried Secret of the Whistling Teeth!' I said.

'Maybe you can be treasure seekers and find it,' said Birdy, with a grin.

'We're good at that,' said Beans. 'We're the Mystery Squad!' And she started telling Birdy all about us. I wasn't sure it was a very good idea. Birdy was Mr Silver's friend but even so we were supposed to be on a Top Secret Mission. The trouble was I had to keep my eye on what I was doing, or we'd have gone crashing into the rocks, like the *Mary Estelle*.

'That's Deadman's Cove ahead,' Birdy said. 'It's the only decent anchorage on the island.'

'Deadman's Cove?'

'The wreckers were killed and their bodies were thrown off the cliff there,' said Birdy. 'It's supposed to be haunted. There are noises at night . . . an eerie whistling . . .'

'That's the wind in the caves,' Beans said.

'Y-e-s,' said Birdy. 'So some say. I'd not care to test it, would you?'

'No fear!' said Beans.

I thought Birdy was teasing us, the way she said it.

We moored about fifty metres away from the Divers' boat, but there was no sign of them.

'Where are you planning to camp?' Birdy asked, when we were all safe on the beach.

'Somewhere with good cover and a fresh water source, if we can,' said James.

'There's a stream by North Point,' said Birdy.

'Where's that?'

'I'd better draw you a map.'

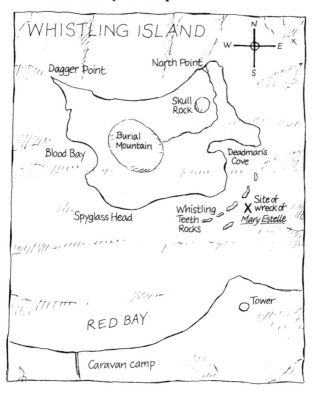

'Gosh!' said Beans, looking at it.

'Blood Bay! Spyglass Head! Deadman's Cove!' I said.

'Don't get all excited, Bodge,' said James. 'Just give me a hand to hump some of this gear.'

Birdy showed us the way up from Deadman's Cove to the stream that led across North Point. We passed the Skull Rock, which really looked like a skull.

'Creepy,' said Beans.

We all thought it was. We were going to camp close to the North Point, where the stream met the sea, and we weren't sorry to leave the Rock behind us.

'Can you manage the tents all right?' Birdy said, when she'd shown us the best place.

'We're very good at managing,' I said. 'Honest we are.'

'Well . . . don't go being chased by dead wreckers, will you?' she said. 'It's not every island has a haunted cove.'

'Haunted by dead lobsters,' muttered Casey. 'Killed off by rotten power stations!'

'There's treasure too!' I said.

'I ought to stay with you . . .' Birdy said.

'No,' said James and Casey, together. Then they both went red.

'I mean, we don't want to be rude,' said Casey, quickly, 'but this is supposed to be our camp, you know? Just for kids.'

'It's an adventure for us,' said James.

They were making it sound like kid's stuff, but I knew what they were up to. Our real mission on the island was to spy on the Devil Divers and we couldn't do that with Birdy hanging round us.

'Well . . . look,' said Birdy. 'I don't think you should be left totally alone. I mean, supposing one of you had an accident?'

'We can cope,' said Casey.

'I'm sure you can. The Mystery Squad on Treasure Island, eh?' said Birdy. 'I don't want to interfere with your lovely adventure.'

'You wouldn't be interfering, not exactly,' said Beans, awkwardly. 'It's just, well . . .'

'You want to be on your own,' said Birdy, with a grin. She had a cheerful face. 'Okay! You win. I'll stay down in the cove, on the *Morning Dew*. Then if you do have any trouble, you can call me.'

'Well . . . er . . .' Casey hesitated.

'No trouble!' said Birdy. 'Off I go, as ordered!' and off she went, leaving us all feeling we'd been rotten rude.

'MSM time!' I said.

'No Mystery Squad Meetings till we've moved camp!' said Casey.

'What?'

'We don't want the Divers to spot us, if we can help it, remember?'

'And?'

'And I reckon this is one of their camp sites,' said Casey.

'Fresh water nearby, signs of a fire,' James said. 'But it's not necessarily the Divers' camp, Casey, is it?'

'Porky's been up here,' said Casey.

'Porky?'

'The fat Devil Diver. He's been up here, but he's not very good at covering his tracks!'

What has Casey spotted?

A footprint? Turn to **10**.

A stub of one of Porky's cigars? Turn to **62**.

A piece of paper with Porky's name on? Turn to **53**.

75

You might be able to attract help, but the tower is far away from the caravan camp, and by the time help reaches you . . . ? Try again. Turn to **59**.

76

Wrong. Turn to **47** and try again.

77

Wrong! Move on to **51**.

78

Wrong. Turn to **70** and try again.

79

Wrong! Go to **48**.

80

It wouldn't work . . . but why? If you need a clue, turn to **44**. If not, turn to **15**.

81

Casey was wrong. Turn to **6**.

82

Porky and who?
Was it another Diver? Turn to **64**.
Was it Casey's dad? Turn to **55**.
Was it Birdy Hamill? Turn to **27**.
Was it Mr Silver? Turn to **18**.

83

Wrong! Go to **48**.

The Mystery Squad Detective Rating

This chart will show you the Detective Rating you've earned by completing this Solve it Yourself Mystery.

You should be able to improve your score as you tackle further mysteries in the series and pick up more tips from them. Keep a note of your scores for future reference.

Your Score	*Detective Rating*
60-70	Sherlock Holmes!
50-59	Super Sleuth!
40-49	Ace Detective
30-39	Detective—1st Class
20-29	Detective—2nd Class
11-19	Junior Detective
6-10	Trainee
0-5	Beginner

If you've enjoyed reading this Solve it Yourself Mystery and would like to test your detective skills further, here are some more titles in the same series:

The Mystery Squad and the Dead Man's Message
The Mystery Squad and the Artful Dodger
The Mystery Squad and Mr Midnight